W9-BMA-902

Noodles and the Bully

Look for picture clues on page 26
to help you read this book.

No part of this publication may be reproduced, stored in a retrieval system, or transmitted in any form or by any means, electronic, mechanical, photocopying, recording, or otherwise, without written permission of the publisher. For information regarding permission, write to Scholastic Inc., Attention: Permissions Department, 557 Broadway, New York, NY 10012.

Copyright © 2012 by Hans Wilhelm, Inc.

All rights reserved. Published by Scholastic Inc.
SCHOLASTIC, NOODLES, and associated logos
are trademarks and/or registered trademarks of Scholastic Inc.
Lexile is a registered trademark of MetaMetrics, Inc.

ISBN 978-0-545-34499-9

12 11 10 9 8 7 6 5 4 3 2   12 13 14 15 16 17/0

Printed in the U.S.A. 40 • First printing, January 2012

Noodles and the Bully

by Hans Wilhelm

SCHOLASTIC INC.

New York   Toronto   London   Auckland
Sydney   Mexico City   New Delhi   Hong Kong

 wants to play.

"Let's go to the park," says .

"We can play with my ."

"Okay," says Scottie.

He hides his .

Then the  walk to the park.

On the way, the  see Tank.

"Give me that ⬤!" says Tank.
"No," says 🐕. "It's *my* ⬤.
But you can play with us."

"I don't play with little ," says
Tank.

He grabs the  and walks away.

"Let's go to the park," says .

 loves to .

So does Scottie.

They each jump on a .

"Yippee!" cries .

"This is fun!"

"I'm flying," says Scottie.

"Get down!" yells Tank. "That
is *my* !"
"No, it's not!" says .

"You heard me, little !"

says Tank. "Get off

my ."

"Let me go!" cries .

"That bully always picks on small ," says . The walk toward the slide.

Scottie goes first.

"Wee!" he yells as he slides down.

 goes next.

But Tank is waiting for him.

"You tripped me!" cries .

"This is *my* slide," says Tank.

"This is no place for little ."

"That bully is mean," says .
"He took my . He took my .
He even took the slide."

"And there is nothing we can do,"

says Scottie.

"That's not true!" says .

"I have an idea!"

 runs toward Tank.

Then he grabs the ⬤.

"That's *my* 🏀!" cries Tank. "Give it back!"

"Catch me if you can!" yells 🐕.

The bully runs after .

But is fast.

He drops the into a hole.

Tank jumps into the hole. He wants

his  back.

He is in for a big surprise!

"Yuck!" cries Tank. "A !
HELP!"

It is too late.

The  is not scared of Tank.

The  sprays him from top to bottom.

Tank runs away as fast as he can.

He should have shared the

and the and the slide.

"Sharing is fun," says .

"But bullies really stink!"

There are six picture clues in this book. Did you spot them all?

Try reading the words on the following pages. If you need help, turn the page. The pictures on the other side will be your clue.

Reading is fun with Noodles!

Noodles

---

ball

bone

---

dogs

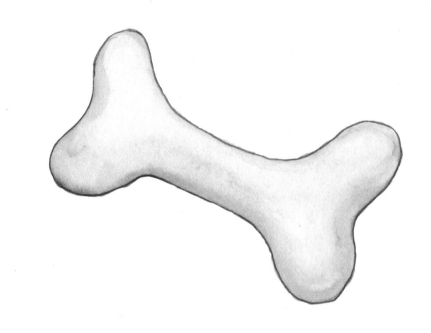

swing

---

skunk